Nintendo + ILLUMINATION

THE SUPER MARIO BROS. MOVIE

OFFICIAL ACTIVITY BOOK

Random House 🏠 New York

Published in the United States by Random House Children's Books, a division of
Penguin Random House LLC, 1745 Broadway, New York, NY 10019, and in Canada by
Penguin Random House Canada Limited, Toronto. Random House and the colophon
are registered trademarks of Penguin Random House LLC.
ISBN 978-0-593-64603-8 (trade)
rhcbooks.com
Printed in the United States of America
10 9 8 7 6 5 4 3 2 1

Bring On the Bad Guy!

All is not well in the Ice Kingdom. A powerful leader and his massive army are attacking! To find out the name of the bad guy, write the letter that comes before each of the letters below on the blanks.

| C | P | X | T | F | S |

See all answers on pages

Bow Before Bowser!

Bowser is King of the Koopas.
He's big and scary and travels in his huge airship—
which holds his whole army! Use the grid to help you draw Bowser.

Bowser wants to take over all the other kingdoms!
He finds the strongest Power-Up ever in the Ice Kingdom.
Whoever has it becomes invincible! To discover the name
of the Power-Up, start at the arrow and, going clockwise,
write every other letter in order on the blanks.

_____ ____ ____ ____ ____ ____   ____ ____ ____ ____ ____

It's-a Me, Mario!

This is Mario. He lives in New York City and dreams
of becoming the best plumber in town!
Use the grid to help you draw him.

Spot the Differences

Mario and his brother, Luigi, are ready to go on their next plumbing job in New York City. Look at the top picture. Can you find and circle four differences in the bottom picture?

Pipe Maze

Most of the city's pipes are regular, but Mario and Luigi
learn that one special pipe leads to another world!
To reveal the name of the place Mario discovers, follow the maze
of pipes and write the correct letters in each connecting box.

HOSMMOUR

NIMKDOG

I Fear Nothing!

Mario meets Toad. He is a brave resident of the Mushroom Kingdom. Toad is loyal to Princess Peach and would do anything for her.

To find the words that describe Toad, look up, down, backward, and diagonally in the puzzle.

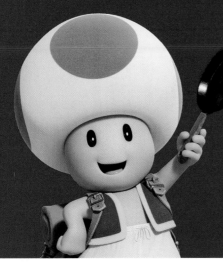

**ADORABLE • CHEERFUL
FRIENDLY • EAGER
TRUSTWORTHY • RELIABLE
ADVENTUROUS • BRAVE**

A	D	O	R	A	B	L	E	W	E	S	R
T	T	U	I	O	P	F	E	E	U	C	C
F	A	R	O	M	B	C	D	O	M	N	H
U	R	H	U	O	P	W	R	E	T	N	E
G	K	I	P	S	T	U	D	A	I	P	E
N	B	V	E	P	T	X	O	E	Q	I	R
D	E	P	T	N	E	W	R	V	A	D	F
V	O	C	E	O	D	N	O	M	K	I	U
D	P	V	E	V	R	L	J	R	P	E	L
L	D	A	E	R	A	P	Y	B	T	M	D
A	R	E	A	G	E	R	N	J	P	H	D
O	E	R	E	L	I	A	B	L	E	E	Y

Spot the Differences!

Look at the top picture. Can you find
and circle five differences in the bottom picture?

She Can Do Anything!

The Mushroom Kingdom is ruled by a kind and strong leader. To discover her name, solve the maze and write the letters along the correct path in order on the blanks.

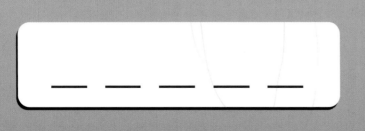

__ __ __ __ __ __

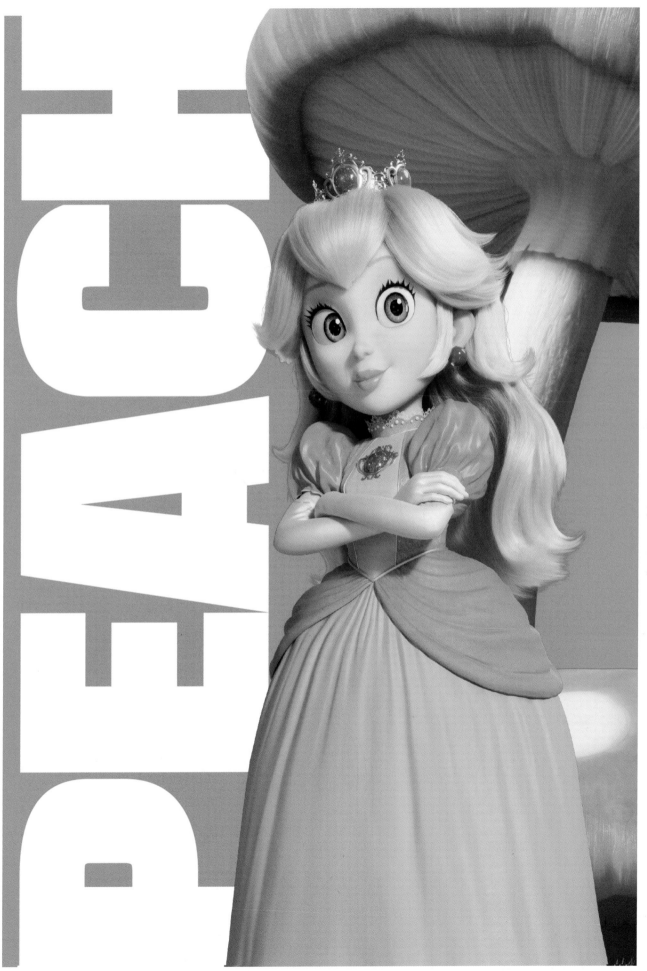

PEACH

Time to Power Up!

Question Boxes hold all kinds of surprises, from
Gold Coins to Mushrooms that make you grow or shrink.
With a friend, take turns drawing a line to connect two dots.
If a line you draw completes a box, give yourself two points.
If your box contains a Question Mark, give yourself three
points for getting the Power-Up! Whoever has more
points after all the boxes have been completed wins!

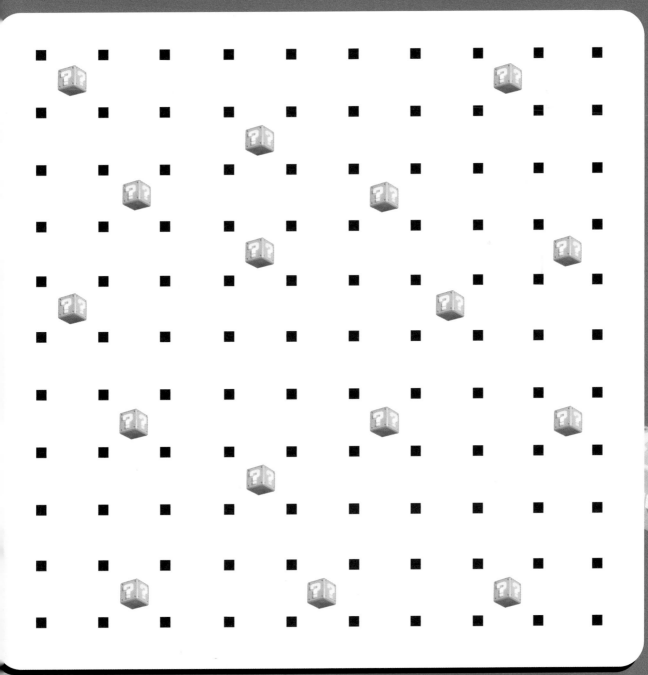

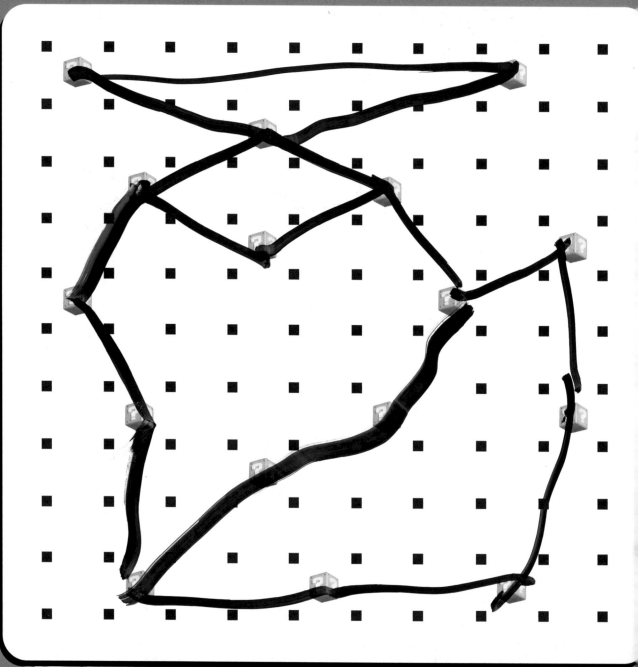

Too Many Koopas!

Koopa Troopas are the foot soldiers in Bowser's army.
Together they can become a real threat—because
there are so many of them! How many Koopa
Troopas can you count here?

Bowser's Most Loyal Henchman

This Koopa is Bowser's advisor and a master of dark magic. To discover his name, cross out each letter of the alphabet that appears in order. Write the remaining letters on the blanks.

_ _ _ _ _ _ _ _ _ _

_ _ _ _ _ _ _ _

A Hero Like No Other!

To master Power-Ups, one must learn to navigate Princess Peach's training course without running into any Piranha Plants. Help Mario get through it unscathed!

FINISH

START

The Super Star is the most powerful Power-Up ever!
It can make you invincible. If you could have any
Power-Up, what would it be? Draw it!

KING OF THE KOOPAS

BOWSER

Watch Out, Luigi!

Luigi got separated from Mario and landed in a dark and creepy place in Bowser's territory! Help him get to the other side and avoid all the Koopa Troopas.

FINISH

START

27

Power-Up Again!

With Bowser taking over more and more kingdoms, look out for Power-Ups! Using the code below, write down the names of all the Power-Ups.

S⬤P⬤R ST★R

_____

S⬤P⬤R M⬤SHR⬤⬤M

_____

M⬤N⬤ M⬤SHR⬤⬤M

_____

F⬤R⬤ FL⬤W⬤R

_____

⬤C⬤ FL⬤W⬤R

_____

★ = A   ⬤ = I   ⬤ = E   ⬤ = O   ⬤ = U

28

Learn the Power-Ups!

To defeat Bowser and his army, you'll have to master each Power-Up and the abilities they give you. Match each Power-Up with its power.

Allows you to throw fireballs!

Allows you to throw iceballs!

Allows you to grow
super big and strong!

Allows you to shrink
to be super tiny!

I'm Donkey Kong!

Draw a picture of Donkey Kong,
and then color him like the picture below.

OUR BIG ADVENTURE BEGINS NOW!

New Allies

Help Mario get through the maze to reach Donkey Kong!

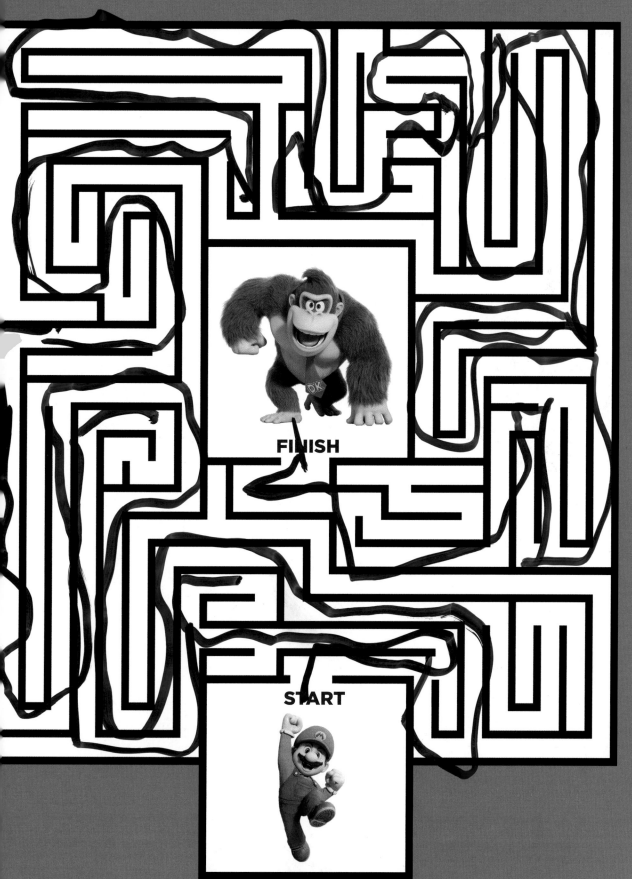

FINISH

START

Mario and his friends create awesome Karts to catch and defeat Bowser. Draw your own Kart to help save the day!

Home, Sweet Home!

To get back home, Mario and Luigi must travel through pipes, but it's been a long adventure for the brothers. Remind them where they're going by following the maze of pipes and writing the correct letters in each box.

E R W

Y O K N

The *Super Mario Bros. Movie* Poster!

Have an adult help you carefully remove the next four pages and trim the edges. Lay them facedown in the correct order. Tape the pages together and hang the poster on your wall— then flip it over later to enjoy the poster on the other side!